My Brother Stevie

OTHER YEARLING BOOKS YOU WILL ENJOY:

My Brother Stevie

Eleanor Clymer

A Yearling Book

Published by
Dell Publishing
a division of
Bantam Doubleday Dell Publishing Group, Inc.
666 Fifth Avenue
New York, New York 10103

The trademark Yearling® is registered in the U.S. Patent and Trademark
Office.

The trademark Dell® is registered in the U.S. Patent and Trademark Office.

ISBN: 0-440-40125-9

Printed in the United States of America

January 1989

10 9 8 7 6 5 4 3 2

CWO

Contents

I'm Annie Jenner

THE LAST THING MY MOTHER SAID TO ME WAS, "TAKE care of your brother."

I wished she hadn't. I suppose I would have anyhow, but it made me mad to think of her saying it. Because why should I have to take care of him, just because I'm his sister? Why shouldn't somebody take care of me? Of course I'm older, but I didn't want to be older. It seemed like it wasn't fair to be punished for something you had no say about.

Well, that's what my mother said. Then she went away. She was always going away, even before Pa died, and leaving us with Grandma. And this time she just went away for good. I didn't know where, and when I used to ask Grandma she would get mad and say, "Don't talk to me about her. Just you and Stevie behave yourselves and

1

grow up decent. I brought up my son, and now he's dead and I have to bring up you."

The trouble was, Grandma didn't ever like Mama. Mama used to sing and dance a lot. She sure could dance. When she was home, she'd be singing and fooling and joking all the time. She'd grab us and kiss us any time she felt like it. But Grandma didn't like that kind of thing.

And sometimes it seems as if she doesn't like Stevie. I guess it's because he's like Mama. He always liked to fool and joke, even when he was real little. He was always full of the devil. Grandma said, "Act nice, sit still, keep clean." But Stevie would act silly, jump around, make everybody laugh. I'd like to be like that too, only I can't. I always had to behave, or else he'd get even sillier and Grandma would smack him.

Like the time Grandma got a new hat for Sunday, and Stevie put it on and put a towel around him for a skirt and paraded around. I laughed and put on my hat and we both paraded like grown-up ladies. Then Grandma came in and grabbed Stevie and whipped him, and then she smacked me too and said, "You're supposed to set a good example."

It wasn't so much fun after Mama went away. Just helping Grandma and minding Stevie and going to school. I don't mean I mind going to school. I like it. It gives you something to do every day—I mean something you have to do. I like getting up and getting ready and going out. Lots of other people are going out too—men and ladies going to work, kids going to school, people opening the stores and sweeping the sidewalk. You feel like you're part of it.

I like to go early so I can see my friends, have time to talk. Then we go in and start to work, see if we know our homework and that. I like when I get to do an example on the board, and the teacher says, "That's very good, Annie."

After school we'd play, then we'd come in and Grandma would give us supper. Whoever came in first could eat first, and then I'd do my homework.

Stevie would watch me do my homework—that was before he went to school himself. He used to be a terrible copycat when he was little. He wanted to do everything I did. He'd take a pencil and try to do homework too. In fact, he could almost read before he went to school, just from copying me.

That was all right, but some things weren't because he didn't understand. Like one time when I was selling raffle tickets for the church, and he took a book and went around scribbling in it, and people gave him pennies because he was so cute. Then Grandma smacked him for begging. But he wasn't really begging. He just wanted to do what I did.

Then when he got bigger, he stopped copying me and started copying other kids. He started to run around with some kids in the building, and they would fool with the washing machines, or sneak into the storeroom if the super forgot to lock it, or jam something into the phones so the dimes would come out.

Grandma would ask me where he was, and I'd say he was playing in the street. I thought I had to cover up for him, or he would be getting lickings all the time.

One day one of the neighbors told Grandma she saw Stevie in the subway with some other kids, fooling with the candy machines. Grandma asked him what he was doing there, and he said he never went there. It must have been somebody else.

Grandma believed him, but when she wasn't looking he gave me a grin. I went in the bedroom later and said, "Stevie, were you in the subway?" He said no. I halfway believed him. Seemed like I couldn't stand the idea of him lying to me. I asked him who he was playing with, and he said Mike.

Mike is a kid about twelve. He's in my grade in school, only not the same class. I told Stevie he'd better stay away from Mike, but he didn't. I couldn't watch him all the time, could I? Once in a while I like to go out with my own friends.

Anyhow, Stevie started going with this bunch of boys. He was younger than the rest, only eight, but he was smart and could run fast, and besides he could always mke people laugh.

For instance one time I was going to the store and I saw a crowd of people. I went over to see, and there was Stevie in the middle, dancing, and the people were laughing and giving him money. He was pretty funny. I had to laugh myself.

Then all of a sudden I saw a lady push through the crowd and grab him. It was Grandma. Was she mad! She pulled him out of there and smacked him so hard I thought she'd half kill him.

I think it was right about then that I started worrying that he would really get in trouble.

One day—it was Saturday—I was going downtown with my friends. I have these friends, Betty and Mary and Doris. I like them all, but Betty is really my best friend. We used to go downtown and look in the store windows and shop in the five and ten. We have a five and ten uptown, but the downtown ones are better. They have different stuff, not so much junk.

We were sitting in the subway train waiting for it to go, and all of a sudden Betty said, "Hey Annie, there's your brother!"

I said where? and looked out the window, and there was a bunch of kids trying to break a candy machine, and there was Stevie in the middle. I saw Mike too. I jumped up and was going to run out, but the doors closed and I couldn't. I banged on the glass, but just then a guard came and the kids all ran away.

So I went on downtown with the girls, but I couldn't really enjoy it. I kept seeing Stevie there in the subway. When I got home I said to him, "Where were you today?" And he said, "In the park." I said, "You mean the subway?" And he said, "No. Why'd you think I was in the subway?"

So then I knew he was lying, but I didn't say any more. It was like, if I acted as if I believed what he said, maybe it would be better. But it wasn't.

The next thing, they started throwing things at trains. See, the railroad goes past the project. And some of these kids go up on the roofs and throw things at the trains, and nobody can catch them. So they think they're real smart. This kid Mike had an air gun, and he hit a window in a train once, and thought it was funny the way the people jumped up and got excited. I heard him telling about it in recess. You could hurt somebody that way, but they never thought of that.

Well, I was worried. I didn't know what to do. "Take care of your brother." That's all right to say, only I didn't know how. I'd yell at him, but it wasn't any use; he got so he didn't even hear what you said to him. And it was no use telling Grandma; she didn't know what to do with him any more than I did.

I got so worried, I got my schoolwork all wrong. I just couldn't pay attention to it.

Stevie was getting so he didn't care what anybody said. They'd send home notes from school about how he disturbed the class, getting up from his seat and running all around and talking and making the kids laugh. That's really what he liked, making everybody laugh, because that meant they liked him.

I could remember when he was a little baby and I was about four or five, and Mama would let me hold him, and he was so soft and warm and nice to hold, and fun to play with. And I thought, why do babies have to grow up and get mean and do bad things and get in trouble, just because they still want somebody to like them and play with them?

So I could understand how he felt. But still when he'd do something bad I couldn't help yelling at him, and that just made him mean. I thought he ought to have a little brother to look out for. All he had was a teddy bear, and Grandma finally threw it out because it was so dirty. I didn't know what to do. I just stayed home; I hardly had any time for my friends at all.

Well, then something lucky happened. Stevie was in the third grade and they had this new teacher. Miss Stover, her name was. I saw her in the hall, and she was real pretty. Stevie came home and told Grandma and me, "I have a new teacher." Grandma said, "Well, you behave now, and don't get fresh to her."

I wanted to tell her that that was the wrong thing to say; it would just make him do some fresh thing, like make faces or tell jokes to get the kids laughing.

So I was waiting for a note to come to tell Grandma the teacher wanted to see her. But nothing came. So I figured, well, the new teacher isn't on to him yet, but just wait.

But still nothing happened. Stevie went to school, and he'd come home and do homework, and play or watch TV, and I was starting to think maybe I could go downtown on Saturday, because Betty and the rest were going to the show. I was thinking about what I would wear, when bingo! it happened.

It was a Thursday afternoon, and starting to get dark. It was only March, so it wasn't spring yet; and Grandma was out, and I was home by myself wondering where Stevie was, and the bell rang. And there was a strange man with Stevie. He had hold of him so he couldn't get away and I said "What happened?"

Stevie didn't say a word. He didn't grin at me the way he does, but just looked at the floor. And the man said, "Is this your brother?"

I said yes, and he said, "Is your mother home?"

I said, "No, we live with our grandmother."

And the man said, "Well, where's she?"

I said, "She's out. What did he do?"

And he said, "These kids were up on my roof. I'm the super from next door. They were throwing rocks at trains. This is the only one I could catch. When's your grandmother coming home?"

I said, "I don't know."

He said, "Well, I can't wait, but I have your address, and let me tell you if I catch him again, it will be too bad."

8

I said, "Please, mister, don't do anything. I'll take care of Stevie."

"You give him a good licking," he said, and went away.

I was so scared I was shivering. This was the first time anybody'd caught him, but I thought next time it could be a cop. I think the man only wanted to scare Stevie and find out if he really lived where he said he did. He could see our apartment was clean and we lived in the project, and that's why he went away so soon. But what was I going to do?

Stevie said, "Are you going to tell Grandma?"

I said, "No, it would just make her mad. But how can I stop you from going with those kids?"

He said, "I dunno. They want me to come, so I do. Anyhow, I like to watch the trains."

I said, "But can't you watch the trains without throwing rocks at them?" And he said, "I dunno. Those people sitting there look so silly." And then he wouldn't say another word.

I thought, "What can I do? Who can I talk to?" And all of a sudden I had an idea. Miss Stover. Only how could I do it without Stevie knowing?

The next day I said to Grandma, "I have to go to school early and help my teacher." And I got out of the house before Stevie was even up. I ran to school and stood by the teachers' gate till Miss Stover came, about a quarter past eight. I thought she might be mad, but I ran up to her and said, "Miss Stover, could I talk to you?"

9

And she turned around and wasn't mad at all. She smiled at me. I remember she had on a red dress and coat, and no hat, and the wind was blowing her hair.

"What's your name?" she said.

I said, "I'm Annie Jenner, I'm Steven's sister, and I have to talk to you, please, Miss Stover. It's about Stevie."

She said, "Come in," and took my arm, and right away I knew why Stevie liked her. She made you feel as if she liked you.

So I told her about Stevie throwing rocks, and I said, "I don't want Grandma to know because she'll only get mad and hit him, and that makes him worse. But could you think of something?" I said, "He told me he likes the trains, but still he throws rocks at them. He could kill somebody!"

She nodded her head yes, and said, "You're right, Annie. I'm glad you told me. You know your little brother is a very bright boy, and it doesn't do any good to hit him."

I said I wished I knew what *would* do some good, and she said, "I know how you feel, Annie. I had to take care of my little brother when my mother died." Then she sort of sighed and said, "Now don't worry, but come and see me again and maybe we can help Stevie." And she smiled again and I felt like hugging her, only I didn't dare. But when I walked out of the room, I felt like I had been carrying a big weight and it was gone.

So that afternoon when Stevie came home, I went in the kitchen and gave him a peanut-butter sandwich and a glass of milk. I waited awhile, but didn't say anything, and at last he said, "My teacher is gonna take us on a train."

I said, "She is? How come?"

He said, "She knows all about trains. She rides on them a whole lot. And we're gonna do trains for social studies, and see a movie about them, and go to the station, and maybe have a ride."

I said, "Gee, that's great, I wish I could go too."

He said, "It's only for our class, but I could ask her—"

I said, "No, you better not, because then all my friends would want to go, and that would be too much. You could maybe tell me about it."

And he said okay.

From then on he was drawing pictures of trains, and cutting out pictures and pasting them up, and playing train in the house with chairs. I didn't hear about throwing rocks anymore; all I heard was "choo choo choo," and why trains are important and how they work.

The only thing was, they didn't really get to ride on the train because it cost too much. But they went to the station and walked through a train after it had stopped, and sat in the seats, so they knew how it looked inside. They brought back posters, and Stevie had one in his room.

Stevie said when they saved up enough money

11

they would go for a ride. And I said, if I got any money from baby-sitting I would give him some. And he was so good, I started thinking maybe I could go out with Betty and the rest, and wondered how I would fix my hair and if I could get some new shoes.

But then something else happened. It wasn't a bad thing, it only meant I had to stick around.

It was Saturday, and I had to help Grandma, take the wash to the launderette and go to the store, and I made Stevie help me. Grandma won't use the washing machines in the building. She thinks they aren't clean enough. Stevie was pushing the shopping cart with all the dirty clothes, when all of a sudden he let out a yell, "Hey! There's my teacher!"

And there she was, walking along with a dog on a leash. It was a cute little dog, brown with white feet, and Stevie looked as if he wanted to pat it, but first he looked up at Miss Stover to see if he should.

She said, "Hello Annie, hello Steven, this is Skipper. Sit, Skipper." The dog sat down. Then she said, "Ask him to shake hands." And Stevie did, and the dog held out his paw.

Well, I thought that was pretty cute. But Stevie! He just sat down on the sidewalk and hugged the dog, and the dog washed his face with its tongue. You could see they just loved each other right away.

12

Miss Stover laughed. She said, "Poor Skipper! At home he has lots of children to play with, but here he's alone most of the time. Maybe I shouldn't have brought him, but I like to have him for company."

I wondered what she meant by "at home." Wasn't she at home here? Then she said, "Stevie, do you want to take Skipper for a little walk while I go into the store?"

"Yes, ma'am," said Stevie. "I'll take care of him."

Miss Stover said, "Oh, but I forgot, you're helping your sister."

"Oh, that's all right," I said. "I'll just put the wash in the machine and be right back. Then Stevie can help me with the groceries."

Well, that was the beginning. After that, Miss Stover let Stevie take Skipper for walks after school. I was surprised that she lived so near us. See, we lived in the project, and she lived in the co-op a few blocks away, and that's how come we saw her going to the store, because we all went to the same supermarket.

Stevie sure did love that dog. Miss Stover would've let him take Skipper home, only Grandma wouldn't have animals in the house getting the floor dirty.

My friend Betty's mother didn't mind, so if the weather was bad we would take Skipper up in her house, and he was a really cute dog. He knew lots of tricks. You could hide a cooky and he would find it. And he'd roll over and play dead dog, and walk on his hind legs. And when he was tired he'd jump in Stevie's lap and snuggle down, and they'd both be happy.

One week end Miss Stover had to go away, and she said to me, "Annie, I'd like to have Steven take care of Skipper for the week end. Do you think your grandmother would possibly let him take Skipper home for a little while?"

I said I would ask. Grandma didn't want to, but she didn't like to refuse the teacher. I promised her I wouldn't let the dog make a mess, and we would keep him in Stevie's room the whole time. Miss Stover said if there was any trouble we should take Skipper to her house, and her super would put him in the apartment and feed him. She could have done that anyhow, but Skipper would have been lonesome, and he'd be happier with children.

The first day Skipper was good, and Stevie spent the whole day in the room with him, except when he took him out. He talked to him. He said, "Hiya, Skipper. How do you like it here? You hungry? Wait there, I'll get you something."

They wrestled on the floor, and I heard growls and giggles. Then it was quiet, and I peeked in and there they were, both sound asleep on the bed.

But after a while, Skipper got to wondering what was in the other part of the house. He got out and found the garbage pail, and got the stuff all over the floor. I heard Stevie yelling for me, and I ran and cleaned it up before Grandma could see it.

But then he got in Grandma's room and found her slipper and chewed one. We couldn't hide that. I took a dollar of my money and bought some new slippers. She scolded me and said by rights Stevie should pay for it, but I was glad he was having a good time, and anyhow he didn't have any money.

But you see why I couldn't go downtown. I had to stick around and keep an eye on things.

But I was feeling better about everything and Grandma wasn't mad at Stevie, and when I did my homework I could even pay attention to the lesson, and my teacher said to me, "Annie, you see what you can do when you try."

I thought to myself, "She doesn't understand much, but Miss Stover does."

And at night when I was in bed I would think about Miss Stover and pretend I was going to do something wonderful for her, like save her from an accident or find her long-lost mother for her. And she would say, "Annie, how can I ever thank you?" And I would say, "Don't try, Miss Stover, after all you did for us."

I Have to Make a Plan

WELL, ONE DAY STEVIE CAME HOME AND HE WAS IN A
real bad mood.

"What's the matter?" I said.

"Nothing," he said, and gave the table a kick.

"Quit that," I said. "What's eating you? Go inside and do your homework."

"I haven't got any homework," he said.

"You're a liar," I said. "Miss Stover gave you
work."

"She did not," he said. "She isn't even there."

"What do you mean?" I asked.

Then he said Miss Stover was absent, and they
had a substitute.

I said she must be sick, and we would go to her
house and take Skipper out for her. So we went,
but she wasn't home, and the super told us she had

16

gone someplace and taken Skipper with her in a suitcase.

What could that mean? I couldn't understand it.

Well, the next day the principal came into Stevie's room and told the class that Miss Stover would be absent for a couple of weeks because her mother was very sick, and she sent them a message to be good children and obey the substitute, and when she came back she would have a surprise for them.

Well, when Stevie came home and told me that, I could understand why Miss Stover took Skipper along, but I couldn't understand about her mother being sick. She told me herself her mother was dead. I thought maybe the principal made a mistake. I wished I had the nerve to go and ask him. Then I thought maybe I'd made a mistake that time and not heard her right.

I worried so much I even dreamed about it at night. I dreamed I saw Miss Stover standing there in her nightgown, as if she had been sick, and I said, "Miss Stover, are you sick?" And she said, "No, it's my mother. Skipper chewed her slippers." Then I woke up and thought what a crazy dream.

Well, I was going crazy in the daytime too, because, see, the principal said she would be gone two weeks. But to a kid like Stevie, only eight and a half, he doesn't understand what two weeks means. As far as he knows, it could be two years, it could be forever.

So he started acting up again. He watched TV all the time and didn't do his homework. He was bad in school and the teacher sent home notes. Grandma said if he wasn't good he couldn't watch TV. Then he started playing hookey from school. I would take him to school in the morning, but at lunchtime he would run out of the playground and not show up all afternoon.

One day Grandma said some money was gone from her pocketbook. She asked Stevie if he took it, and he said no, but I knew he was lying. But I said, "Grandma, maybe you lost it."

And Grandma said, "Annie, if there is one thing I don't do it's lose money."

Stevie didn't say a word, but when I went in his room I could smell chocolate.

Then I read in *The News* about some boys walking on the tracks and one of them got electrocuted, and when Stevie didn't come home, I was so worried I thought I would die.

I thought, "If he only had something to take care of, he wouldn't be so wild. Look at me," I thought, "do I ever get a chance to be wild?"

And Betty would say to me, "Come on and go to the show with us, for heaven's sake. You can't be tied down to your brother the rest of your life."

And I would remember, "Take care of your brother." It was like it was the only thing I had left from my mother.

I thought that if we could have Skipper for a few

days it would be nice, and then I got to dreaming again, and I dreamed about writing a letter to Miss Stover and saying could Skipper come to visit us.

Then I thought, why not? I mean, why not write to her? But how could I get her address? I didn't want to ask the substitute, because she would ask me why I wanted to write. If I only had the nerve I would ask Mr. Russo, the principal, but what would I use for an excuse? Finally I had an idea. I went to his office and knocked on the door, and a lady said, "Come in."

It was very quiet in there, with carpet on the floor and nice curtains and pictures. I said could I talk to Mr. Russo and she said what about? And I said, "I have to ask him something. Please."

She was just shaking her head no, when he came out of a door, and I said, "Oh, Mr. Russo, excuse me please, but I have to ask you something."

He said, "What is it?"

And I said, "My brother and me, we used to take out Miss Stover's dog, and now she's absent and Easter is coming and we want to send her an Easter card, so could you tell me her address, please?"

He looked surprised, but he said, "Why, that is a very nice idea," and told the lady to give it to me. She wrote it down on a card: Miss Mary Stover, R.F.D. 1, Hacketsville, N. Y.

I said, "Where is that?"

The lady said, "Why, it's way out in the country. I guess you'd have to take a train to get there."

Then I understood why Stevie said Miss Stover told them she rode on trains. So I said thank you and went away.

That afternoon I wrote the letter. It took me a long time, because I had to cross out a lot and write it over about four times. By then it was too late to mail it, and the next morning I had no time to buy a stamp. I didn't want to take it to school in case I lost it, so I put it in my bureau and bought the stamp in the afternoon, but when I came home and looked for the letter, it was gone.

I asked Grandma if she had seen a letter, and she said, "No, who was it to?"

I said I had sent away for something. I thought to myself, "I am getting to be a worse liar than Stevie." And I felt like giving up the whole thing and letting him grow up and go to jail if he wanted to.

Then Stevie came in, and I asked him if he saw my letter and he said no. But when I went down with the garbage I found a piece of torn envelope, and it was mine. I knew then that Stevie must have taken it and read it, and when he saw it was about him he threw it away; but it was as if something made him leave a little piece, so I'd know.

I felt like hitting him hard, so hard he wouldn't be able to sit down. I thought, that's what he needs. But I knew it wasn't. It might make me feel a little better, but it wouldn't cure him. But I was mad, and I kept saying to myself, "I hate him, I hate him."

I am supposed to look out for him and I don't do anything right, and Grandma doesn't know any more than me, and she says he's no good and will land in reform school, and I guess she hates me too because our mother left us with her. Some girls have fun, I thought, but I never do and never will.

I sat down on a box there in the cellar behind some pipes, and looked at the ashcans and the pipes, and I felt all alone, as if there wasn't another soul in the world but me, and I was going to sit here in this cellar the rest of my life and look at ashcans and hear the elevator door banging.

It was as if I was another person looking at me and feeling sorry for me, and I wanted to cry, and then I did cry. I cried and cried, and hoped nobody would come and make me stop.

But suddenly I heard the elevator door bang open, and I heard laughing and feet shuffling, and I thought, "It's Stevie and his friends, and if they see me with my eyes all red, they'll laugh."

So I hid there and heard them scrabbling around in the trash and saying, "I got a good one!" They were putting things in their pockets, pieces of glass and stuff. And then they ran to the elevator and banged the door shut.

I thought, "I bet I know where they're going. They are going to the roof, and fire rocks and

21

things at the trains." I wondered if I should run after them, or tell Grandma, or the super, or the guard, or just forget it.

If the guard caught them, they'd be in trouble for sure. I thought I'd better follow them. So I ran to the other elevator, but it took a long time coming. Then there were a million people trying to get on, and besides, some kid must have run down the stairs and pushed the buttons at every floor, so it took forever to get to the top. But at last it did, and I ran to the roof.

It was almost dark, and the lights were lit in the street and in the windows, and I could see what looked like a river of cars. It was really two rivers, one way with red lights and one way with white lights. It was real pretty, with the sky so dark blue, only I couldn't think about that then. I didn't see the boys. I thought maybe they changed their minds, but then a train came along, all lit up like a string of beads, and there was a tinkling crash, and I could see people in the train jumping up and down.

Then I heard feet running and two men shouting, "Come here, you little rats!" And there was the sound of a smack and somebody yelling, "Ow! I didn't do it."

Then each man was dragging a kid off by the back of the neck. I couldn't see if Stevie was one of them. But I went down to the apartment. I was shivering and shaking as much as if I had done something, and I hoped I wouldn't see Grandma.

But thank goodness it was Friday night and she had gone to church. They were having Bible class. It was at night, so the working people could come. I thought, "If she's praying for us, I hope it does some good."

I felt awfully thirsty, and I was just taking a drink of water when the door opened and Stevie ran in. He was breathing awful hard, and he flopped down in a chair.

I said, "Are you sick?" He said, "No, I was playing."

I thought, "I'm not hiding this anymore," and I said to him, "Stevie, I know where you were. And if you don't do what I say, I'm going to tell the guards and the cop, and you will go to reform school and never get out."

If he hadn't been so young he would have known I would never really tell a cop. But he was scared, and believed me. So he said, "What do you want me to do?"

I said, "Tomorrow is Saturday, and from now till Monday you are not going to go out of this house unless I say you can."

He said, "All right. I wasn't going out anyhow," bold as anything.

So I gave him some supper that Grandma had left and said, "You eat that now and go to bed, and I'll decide later what you have to do next." And he did.

And I sat in the kitchen and thought, "I fooled

him into it this time, but I have to make a plan, and it better be good."

I sat and thought and thought, and ate a piece of bread, and then I got an idea. The more I thought about it, the hungrier I got, and I finally ate the whole loaf and some peanut butter, and then I drank some water, and by then I had made up my mind. I would take Stevie to see Skipper. I didn't know how I would do it, but somehow I would.

Two Round-Trip Tickets

I WENT INTO STEVIE'S ROOM AND HE WAS IN BED WITH his clothes on, looking at a comic. He wouldn't look at me.

I said, "I'm going out for a while, but you stay here. If Grandma comes, say I went to Betty's and I'll be right back. Did you hear me?"

He didn't answer. He was mad at me.

I said, "Did you *hear* me? Answer me when I talk to you."

He grumbled something and I went out. I took my pocketbook and all the money I had. It was about three dollars. It was what I was saving for new shoes, but I would have to start all over again. I went to Betty's and asked her to lend me some money. I said it was very important, but not to ask me what it was, because it was to keep me out of trouble, and it would be better if she didn't know. So she took every cent she had, about four dollars, and said she wasn't going to the show tomorrow anyhow, she was going to see her aunt. Betty is a real good friend. Then I went to the station.

I walked all the way so as not to waste any money, because I didn't know how much I would need. It was dark, and I was pretty scared, but nobody bothered me, and when I got there I said to the man, "Are there any trains that go to Hacketsville?" and he said, "Tonight?" and I said, "No, tomorrow."

He said yes, and I said, "How much for a ticket?"

He said, "Under or over twelve?" And I said, "One under and one over." So he told me it was $4.00 round trip for over twelve and $2.00 for kids under twelve, and I got two tickets.

Then I went home. I only had about a dollar left, but I took a bus, and when I got off the bus I ran because it was late, and before I got there I was breathing so hard my chest hurt. I went in and held the tickets in my hand, so if anybody grabbed my pocketbook they wouldn't get them, and then I ran in the apartment and in my room and hid them under the mattress.

Grandma was home by then, and Stevie was asleep. Grandma didn't ask me any questions. She was sitting in her chair half asleep with *The News* in her lap, and I thought she looked sort of skinny and old, bent over like that. I thought of what I

26

was going to do, and felt mean, not telling her. But I thought, "I can't tell her. She wouldn't understand."

But the real reason was, she would say it was crazy, and I knew that was true, and that's why I was scared. So I drank some milk and went to bed.

I had some more dreams. I was trying to get someplace and carrying a heavy shopping bag, and it got heavier and heavier, and I was walking and running, and finally I put the bag down, and then I couldn't find it, and I thought I would die if I lost it, and then I woke up in a sweat and thought, "Thank goodness it was only a dream." But then I remembered what I had to do the next day, and wished I was back in the dream.

The next day was Saturday, and it was a nice sunny day. I got up early and said to Grandma, "Is the laundry ready?"

She said, "What's your hurry? You aren't even dressed."

So I said, "I want to take Stevie to the show."

She said, "You do? What's the matter, can't you go with your own friends?"

I said, "Sure, but I thought it would keep him out of mischief."

She looked surprised, but she said all right. She went and got all the wash while I ate my cereal. It tasted so dry I could hardly get it down. I thought, "I better take Stevie with me and not let him out of my sight." So I went in his room and said, "Come on, get up. We have to do the wash."

He rolled over and said, "I don't feel good."

I said, "What's the matter?"

He said, "I got a stomach-ache." I knew it was just because he didn't want to go to the laundry. He'd done it before. So I said, "You get up and help me, and I've got a surprise for you."

"What is it?" he wanted to know.

I said, "I'm going to the show, and you can come. I have some money."

He said, "What show?" And I said "Downtown. But you have to help me, or I won't get done in time."

So then he got up, and we went out and did the wash and went to the store, and all the time I kept wishing it was just a regular day like every other Saturday, and I would wake up and find out I didn't have to go any place but could really go to the show. But I had the tickets pinned inside the pocket of my blouse, and when I looked down and saw the safety pin, I remembered.

So we came home, and I said to Stevie, "Now you wash your face and put on your good pants, because I'm not taking you if you look like a tramp."

Then I made some sandwiches and put them in a bag, and put on my good dress, and said good-bye to Grandma. She gave me a funny look and said, "Wait."

She took her pocketbook and took out two dollars and said, "Here."

I said, "Thanks, Grandma," and wanted to kiss

her because I knew she couldn't afford it, and I felt as if I was leaving her forever. But she would have thought I was crazy, so I didn't.

Stevie and I went down in the elevator and I started walking, and he said, "Hey, where are you going? That's not the way to the subway." And I said, "This is the real surprise."

I showed him the tickets and said, "We're not going downtown to the show; we're going on a train to see Skipper."

He started to yell, "You're nuts!" and was going to run away from me, but I grabbed him and held on tight and said, "Come on, we can do it. I never was on a train and I always wanted to go, but I thought it wasn't fair to go without you, so come on, because you know more about it than me."

Well, he calmed down, and right away he proved he did know more about it. He said, "Have you got a timetable?"

I said, "No, I didn't even think of it. I thought it was like the subway."

And he said, "Well, if you are so dumb, hurry up. We better take the bus because we might just miss one. They don't run all the time, only maybe every couple of hours."

So we jumped on a bus, and it crawled so slow I thought I would scream. It stopped for every red light, and then it stopped at every corner for people to get on and off, and a taxi would get in the way and while we waited the light would turn red.

But at last it got there, and we jumped off and ran like crazy, and I said to a man, "When is the next train to Hacketsville?"

He said, "One is coming in right now. Run and you might get it."

Well, it was a good thing Stevie had been in the station before, because he knew just where to run, and there was the train making a noise like it was all ready to go, and we jumped in and a man outside waved his arm, and it started.

We sat down all out of breath. Stevie sat next to the window, and I could see he was real excited. He'd been in the train before, but not moving, and here it was really going.

It went faster and faster, and we were going past houses and streets. You could sit there and look right into people's windows. It felt funny, as if we were on the other side of a mirror. I thought, "I could be the person in that window, watching the people in the train going someplace where I never went and seeing things I never would see, and I might feel like throwing a rock at them." I looked at Stevie and wondered if he was thinking the same thing.

We went over a bridge across a river, and then a man came along and said, "Tickets, please."

"This is it," I thought. He might say no kids allowed without grownups and make us get off, and where would we be?

I had an idea. I gave Stevie the tickets and said,

30

"Here, you hand them out," because Stevie still looked real cute when he was good, and the man might be nice to him.

And he was. He winked at Stevie and said, "Yes, *sir!*" He tore them in half and gave Stevie back the other half and said, "Here you are, sir. Don't lose them." And he went on by. Boy, that was a relief!

Then I calmed down and started looking out of the window again. Pretty soon everything was green—trees and grass and bushes with flowers on them. We saw houses with yards around them, and roads with cars speeding. Every time we'd come to cross a road, the train would blow a loud whistle. It really was fun. Then we'd stop at a station and some people would get off. There would be people outside to meet them, and they would stand there kissing each other and hugging, and then get into cars and drive off. I thought it would be nice to have somebody come to meet you and be glad to see you. Too bad Miss Stover didn't know we were coming.

And I noticed a funny thing. The people who came in the cars to meet their friends weren't all dressed up. I thought the ones that lived out here would all be rich, but the ladies had on skirts and sweaters, and the kids were in jeans, and the men were in old pants and shirts. One man had a big hole in his sleeve and his shoes were flapping. Grandma wouldn't let us go out like that, even if she does get welfare. I wondered what kind of houses they lived in.

Then I wondered how we would know when to get off, but Stevie said the conductor would call out the stations, and sure enough, he did, every time we came to one.

At last I heard him shout, "Hacketsville, the next station stop!"

We stood up, and I grabbed my pocketbook and my paper bag, and the train slowed down and we got off.

Then all the people who had come to meet somebody started hugging and kissing and saying, "It's good to see you." And the train started up and went faster and faster till it was gone. All the people got in their cars and went away, and there we were alone.

Apple Pie with My Ice Cream

MY, IT WAS QUIET. I NEVER HEARD ANYTHING SO QUIET.

It was like being deaf. Then I heard Stevie say, "I'm hungry." So we sat down on a bench and ate our sandwiches. Then Stevie got up and looked around the station. It was just a little house painted red, and there was nobody there. But there was a drinking fountain, so we had a drink.

Then Stevie said, "How are we going to find Skipper?" And I thought to myself, "That's a good question. Here it is the middle of the afternoon and not a living soul to ask."

Finally I said, "Maybe there's a store around here. They might have a phone." So we walked up a hill, and there were some houses on a street and a few stores. That made me feel a little better. At least there were some people in this place. So I said, "Come on," and we found a phone booth out in the street with a phone book in it—a little one. I grabbed it and looked for Miss Mary Stover. She wasn't there.

Now what? I was beginning to think Stevie was right and I was nuts, coming out here without letting her know. Stevie stood there looking at me and waiting for me to do something, and I felt scared.

"There's a drugstore," I said. "Let's get a Coke."

We went in and asked for two Cokes. The man looked at us as if he was wondering who we were and where we came from, but he gave us the Cokes and we drank them.

Then I said, "Mister, could you tell us where R.F.D. 1 is?"

He stared at me as if I was talking Chinese.

I said, "We came to see Miss Mary Stover. She lives in Hacketsville, New York. The number is R.F.D. 1."

He said, "R.F.D. 1 isn't a number. It's a post office address."

I said, "Oh. Well, how can I find her?"

He said, "Did you look in the phone book?"

I said, "Yes, but she isn't in there."

He asked me, "Does she know you're coming to see her?"

I said, "I wrote her a letter." I didn't tell him it never got mailed.

He said, "Well, does she live with somebody?"

I said, "Yes, her mother."

He looked puzzled. "Can't help you," he said. "Where did you kids come from?"

I didn't want to say. I said, "Oh, we just came to visit."

Then Stevie spoke up. "She's got a dog named Skipper."

There were some kids standing in the front of the store looking at comics. One of them was about the size of Stevie. He put in his two cents.

"I know a kid has a dog named Skipper. He's in my class."

The man said, "Oh? Where does he live?"

The kid said, "Out Spring Hill. They come on the bus."

The man said, "Oh! I see. What's the kid's name?"

"Johnny Harris."

The man looked in the phone book. Then he said, "No Harris out Spring Hill way. Too bad the post office is closed. Ernie might know."

I was getting awfully tired, and I didn't know what they were talking about. I wished Stevie and I could just get back on the train and go home. At least, at home when they give you an address it means something. I could see Stevie was tired too. He sat on his stool all sort of droopy. I thought, "In a minute he'll fall off." Then I thought, "I brought him here. He said he didn't feel good this morning—what if he gets sick?"

But suddenly the kid pointed out the door and yelled, "There's Ernie now!"

We looked, and there was a postman. He had on a blue uniform and was getting out of a red white and blue truck. At least *that* was the same out here.

The drugstore man yelled, "Hey, Ernie! Come on in here!"

The postman came in. The man said, "Ernie, you know a Miss Mary Stover out Spring Hill way?

I held my breath. Then I let it out again. Ernie was nodding his head yes. He said, "Sure, that's one of Mrs. Carter's girls."

I shook my head. I was ready to cry. I said, "She's not a girl. She's a lady. A teacher."

"That's right," said Ernie. "Why do you want to know?"

The drugstore man said, "These kids came to see her."

Ernie said, "Well, you could phone her, see if she's there. I heard she was back. Mrs. Carter's sick."

The drugstore man looked in the book again under Carter, and this time he found a number. He dialed it. I held my breath again. What if it wasn't Miss Stover? What if she wasn't home? Maybe by now she was back in the city. What made me think of such a dumb thing to do? It only took the man a minute to dial, but it was the longest minute I ever knew. Then I heard him talking. "Miss Mary Stover? This is the Rexall store in town. There's two kids here to see you. I'll let you talk to the girl."

He called me over and said, "Here you are." And I took the phone and said, "Miss Stover?" And my voice was shaking so much I was sure she couldn't hear me. Then I heard her voice, all steady and natural, just the way she always sounded. She said, "Hello! Who is it?"

I said, "This is Annie. Annie Jenner, and I'm here with Stevie. Do you remember us?"

She said, "Of course, Annie, but how in the world did you get there?"

I said, "We came on the train, and now we're in the drugstore. I thought we could find you and just say hello, but I don't know where you are—" and my voice started shaking again.

She said, "Let me talk to the man again, please."

The man got on the phone and talked a little, and then he hung up and said to us, "It's all right. She said to put you kids in a taxi and send you out there."

Ernie and the kids in the store and some other people were all listening by this time, and when he said that about the taxi, they all smiled and nodded their heads as if they were glad, and I thought, "They're nice people."

Then Ernie said to the drugstore man, "You're alone in the store. I'll take them over to the taxi." So we went with Ernie and he put us in a car. It

37

didn't look like a taxi, just a plain car. He told the man, "Take these kids to Carters out on Harley Road, Spring Hill, and they'll pay you when you get there."

"I've got money," I said, though I didn't know if I'd have enough. I didn't know how far it was.

We started out, and what a ride! Up a hill past some big fancy houses with swimming pools and big trees, and I thought, "I wonder if she lives in a house like that. She must have a nice house." Then we passed a church, and some woods, and a field with horses.

Stevie yelled, "Look at the horses!"

Then we came to some smaller houses, with lots of kids playing around and wash hanging out, not fancy at all, and the taxi seemed to be slowing down, and I thought, "This can't be it!" But suddenly the taxi stopped in front of one of the houses and the man said, "Here we are!"

I looked for the meter to see how much it was, because I thought a ride like that must be five dollars, but there was no meter, and I started to ask him when suddenly Stevie opened the door and jumped out. Something little and brown came running at him barking like crazy, and Stevie grabbed it and they rolled on the ground. It was like an explosion, shouting and barking and rolling around. People came running out, and you never saw such a commotion in your life.

I grabbed Stevie up off the ground, but the dog

kept jumping up and licking us both. Then I saw Miss Stover, and she held out her arms to Stevie and he ran into them and hugged her.

Then she kissed me too, and I almost cried, but I didn't. I wished I could be as young as Stevie and run into her arms that way.

She paid the taxi man and said, "Thanks very much"; and I could hardly believe it, it was only a dollar. He drove away grinning and waving his arm out the window. I never saw a taxi man do that before.

Then Miss Stover said, "Well, this is a wonderful surprise!" And I had a good look at her. She didn't look like a teacher at all, she just looked like any grown-up girl. She had on pants and a sweater, and her hair in a ponytail, and no lipstick.

She said, "I'm sorry I didn't know you were coming, or I would have been down to meet you." I thought, "That would have been nice. I would love to be one of the people that gets off the train and has somebody there with a car to meet them."

Then I saw there was a bunch of kids hanging around the side of the house staring at us, and Miss Stover said, "Come here, children, I want you to meet two friends from the city. This is Stevie and this is Annie. Stevie, this is Johnny, and this is Billy, and this is Carol. They live with us. And these others are Mary and Joan and Mike. They live next door. You go and play now, and pretty soon I'll call you to a party."

Then she took me inside and said, "I'll introduce you to my mother, but we won't stay long because she has been sick and isn't very strong yet." She took me into a bedroom, and there was a lady in bed, propped up against the pillows. She wasn't very big. I could see her feet didn't come more than halfway down the bed, and her hair was gray.

Miss Stover said, "Mama, this is Annie Jenner. She brought her little brother out to see us from the city. Don't you think that was smart of her?"

The lady held out her hand and said, "I'm so glad to know you, dear," and her voice was like Miss Stover's, strong and steady, even though she looked pretty weak.

I said, "I'm glad to know you too, Mrs. Stover."

But Miss Stover said, "Mrs. Carter."

Then her mother said, "Mary dear, you'll manage all right, won't you? I think we can put them on the sunporch for tonight."

Miss Stover said, "Of course, Mama. I'll borrow a cot from next door and we'll have a fine time." And she patted her hand and said to me, "Now we'll go and let Mama have a nap, and you'll help me in the kitchen."

I followed her to the kitchen. It was all bright and sunny, with colored glass bottles in the windows and plants all around and a big round table. Miss Stover said, "Now wash your hands there at the sink— or no, I'll give you a towel and you go in the bathroom and wash up—and then we'll fix some food."

40

I went and washed my hands and face—I didn't know I was so dirty and my hair such a mess till I looked in the mirror. There were tear marks and dust on my face, and I felt ashamed of Miss Stover seeing me that way. The cool water felt good, and I just sat on the edge of the tub for a while and rested myself. Then I came out and Miss Stover was talking on the phone. She was saying something like, "I'm sure you can manage very well, and we'll see you another time. I'll tell you all about it when I see you."

All of a sudden I thought, "Suppose she had a date for tonight and we walked in on her!" But she didn't say anything to me about it. When she saw me she said, "Oh, Annie, here's a job for you. Spread peanut butter on this bread for me."

Just as if she was expecting me to come and help her make a party for the little kids. She said, "I know you have a lot to tell me, but I thought we'd wait until later, when we can sit down and talk quietly. But one thing I would like to know, is your grandmother all right?"

I said yes, Grandma was fine. Then she said, "And does she know you are here?"

I shook my head no, and suddenly I felt terribly ashamed. What a thing to do, to come all the way out here without telling Grandma! Of course it was still early and she thought we were at the movies, but what would she think when we didn't get home? She'd be scared to death! I hadn't thought of that. Well, really I did think what she'd say, but I was mainly thinking she would yell at me, and wondering what I could give as an excuse. I never thought she might be worried or scared about us.

I said, "Gee, Miss Stover, I said we were going to the show. I have to let her know. We'll be late getting home, and she'll be wondering where we are."

Miss Stover nodded and said, "Yes, she'll be upset. I know you were upset, or you would have told her, but it isn't too late. We can call her up. It's only three o'olock, so we have time. Now put those sandwiches on a plate, and we'll put out some cookies and milk and take them all out to the yard."

We carried the things out and put them on a table they had in the yard, and called all the kids. Some of them were playing on a slide, and some were swinging, and some were playing hide-and-go-seek. They all came running. You'd think Stevie had lived there all his life. He was just as dirty as the rest of them, and he came running, with Skipper jumping and barking after him. Suddenly I knew what Miss Stover meant about Skipper missing the children. He sure was a happy dog out here.

"Come on, everybody," she said. "Fall to."

They sat down and started cleaning up the sandwiches, and Miss Stover asked Stevie how he liked the train ride. He started telling them all about it, how we didn't have a timetable, but ran and caught the train, and how the conductor swung his arm to tell the engineer to go, and how he stood in the doorway and shouted the station stops. That kid didn't miss a thing.

Miss Stover told them, "You know, Stevie lives right near the railroad. He can go up on the roof and see the trains go by. Don't they look nice all lit up at night, Stevie?"

He said, with his mouth full of bread, "I'm gonna be a train man when I grow up. And anybody that throws rocks at the trains, I'm gonna put them in jail."

"That's right, Stevie," said Miss Stover.

I thought, "That's the first time he ever really *said* anything about throwing rocks."

Then Miss Stover said, "Children, how would you like to have Annie and Stevie stay overnight here with us, if their grandma will let them? Won't that be fun?"

They all said, "Oh boy! Yeah!"

Stevie's face lit up and he said, "And could Skipper sleep with me, the way he did that time?"

"Of course," said Miss Stover. And she told the others about leaving Skipper with us over the week end. Then she said, "Now Annie and I must go and call up their grandmother, and you children play quietly, because Mama is sleeping."

We took the dishes inside, and Miss Stover leaned against the sink and said, "Now, tell me, Annie, what happened? I can see something must have happened, or was going to happen, and you wanted to tell me about it."

So I told her how Stevie had been acting, and about the letter he tore up, and about the boys getting caught, and why I couldn't tell Grandma, and how scared I was about Stevie.

I said, "He's little now, but he's gonna get wild, and what'll happen when he's bigger? I can scare him now, but when he's bigger he won't listen to me."

Miss Stover said, "He's lucky that he has a sister who loves him."

I thought, "I don't love him; he's a pest. I would like to live here with Miss Stover, if only it wasn't for him." But then I thought, "If it wasn't for him, I wouldn't be here. I wouldn't even know her."

I said, "I thought it would be good for him to see Skipper. You know how he loves Skipper. Maybe if Grandma would let us have a dog, and he would have to take care of it, he'd be better."

She said, "Yes, it's good to be responsible for somebody or something, but he's too young for a dog. You see, he couldn't really take care of it. It would be fun for a few days, but then it would be work. That's how it is to have a dog, and children too. You have to be willing to do a lot of hard work. Sometimes you even hate them. You feel like a slave." She smiled when she said that, but she certainly knew how people felt.

44

She said, "If your grandmother loved dogs, it would be all right. But she'd be impatient, and that wouldn't be good for Stevie. He wouldn't learn patience."

I said, "But how can he learn patience? Grandma isn't patient with him."

And she said, "Why, Annie, from you."

I said, "From me!"

And she laughed and said, "Of course. I can see you have the patience of a saint. Now we must call up your grandma. You tell her where you are, and then I'll talk to her. What's the number?"

I really was scared. While she was dialing I felt all squeezed up inside; I could hardly breathe. I could hear the phone ringing, and I thought, "Maybe she won't be home. I hope she won't be home." But then I heard a voice saying "Hello?"

Miss Stover said, "Just a minute," and handed me the phone.

I said, "Grandma?"

She said, "What? Who is it? Speak louder."

I said, "It's me. It's Annie."

She said, "Annie?" and I heard her voice stop. "Annie? Why are you calling? Did something happen? Where are you?"

I said, "Grandma, we're all right; don't be scared. I just want to tell you something."

She said, "Well, what?"

I said, "Grandma, we didn't go to the show. We went for a train ride. You know how Stevie likes trains. I thought it would be good for him. So I took him on a train, and Grandma, where do you think we went? We went to see Miss Stover."

"Who?"

"Stevie's teacher, Miss Stover. We're in her house now."

Grandma said, "My land a living, what next? You're in her house? Where is that?"

I said, "Miss Stover wants to talk to you."

And I handed her the phone. Then Miss Stover talked to Grandma for a long time, and I heard her say things like, "They're wonderful children, Mrs. Jenner. You should be proud of them, especially Annie. She took good care of her little brother. No, it's no trouble. I'm glad to have them. You know, I hated to leave my children, but my mother was so sick. Yes, and I hope when they get home you won't scold them. Yes, she's had a hard time, she's been very frightened."

I wondered who she was talking about. Then she said, "I'll put them on a train tomorrow after dinner. I'm sure they'll get home safely. They've learned a lot. Why, they found out how to travel— that's something."

Then she made me talk some more, and I said, "Grandma, I'm sorry if I scared you." And she said, "Well, it's all right now. Your teacher told me you're all right, and I'll see you tomorrow. And you behave nice now, and see that Stevie does too.

And be sure to tell her thank you. And Annie, do you have enough money?"

I said, "Yes, Grandma, I have, and I have our tickets to come home. Good-bye now."

She said, "Good-bye now," and I hung up, and I felt so weak I had to sit down. I took a couple of deep breaths and said, "Can I have a drink of water?" And Miss Stover brought it to me quick and looked a little scared herself. She said, "Do you feel all right? Do you want to lie down?"

I said, "No, I'm all right, I'm just so glad it's over."

She laughed and said, "Well, it isn't all over, but the worst is over. That's what Mama says."

Suddenly I remembered something I wanted to know. I just had to find out. I said, "Miss Stover, could I ask you something?"

She said, "Of course."

I said, "Don't be mad. I'm not being fresh, but I remember you told me once your mother died. But she's in there."

She said, "Why, Annie, I didn't remember that I said that. You must have been puzzled. Yes, my mother died, and my brother and I were all alone. We were living in a home for children, and he was getting very wild. And then Mama, at least I call her Mama, took us to live with her. She's our foster mother. She brought us up, and she also taught us how to live."

I said, "Your brother too?"

She said, "Yes, he's in college now, learning to be a doctor. He was here only last week to see us."

I said, "And those three kids you said live with you?"

She said, "Yes, they're foster children too. You see, Mama and Papa have no children of their own. So they take care of children who have nobody to take care of them. They've been doing it for a long time. I don't know how many children they've raised. And we love them as much as if they were our own parents."

I said, "Gee, Miss Stover! I never knew about such things!"

And all of a sudden I understood a lot of things. I knew why she was such a good teacher and why the kids liked her. And I knew why she wanted to come home when Mama got sick.

I said, "Are you coming back to school?"

She said, "Annie, that's what I'm worried about. Mama wouldn't want me to give up teaching. She sent me to college to be a teacher. She wanted to go herself and never had a chance. She knows the children need me. But how can I leave her? And how can we send away the children who are here now?"

I said, "I wish I lived here. I'd take care of them for you."

She said, "I wish you could, Annie, but of course you're still a child, and you have to go home and go to school."

I really wished I didn't have to go home, but could stay here always. I looked around at the big clean kitchen and Miss Stover standing by the sink and the colored glass in the window, and thought it would be nice if she would stay here and Stevie and I could come and be foster children. Then she would be our foster mother, and Grandma could take a rest. After all, Grandma's always saying she raised her son and now she has to raise us; maybe she'd be glad.

Of course it was just a daydream.

Just then there was a noise of a truck outside, and I heard heavy footsteps and a man's voice saying, "Anybody home?"

Miss Stover said, "We're in the kitchen, Papa. Come on out and meet my friend."

Then Mr. Carter came in. He was a big tall man with gray hair and a brown uniform. I looked out and saw that the truck was a milk truck.

Miss Stover said, "Papa, this is Annie Jenner. She and her brother Steven came out to see us. Steven was one of my children in the city."

He smiled and held out his hand, and I shook hands with him. His hand was so big it felt like a giant's hand.

He said, "I thought I saw an extra kid out there, but I couldn't be sure how many we had. Glad to meet you, Annie."

Then he said, "How's Mama?"

Miss Stover said, "She's been asleep."

He said, "That's good. I'll look in and see."

And he went to the bedroom. His shoulders were bent over, as if he was tired.

I thought, "It must be nice to have a man like that around the house. I bet Stevie'd do what he said."

Miss Stover said, "Papa's been driving a milk truck for years. He starts to work very early and gets home early, and that way he can be with the children. That's one way they've managed. And besides, he gets the milk cheaper. That helps too."

Then she sighed a little. I could see she had things to worry about besides me and Stevie, and I felt a little ashamed of bothering her.

She said, "Well, Annie, we've got to fix supper. It's nice to have a big girl to help me. I guess we'll have meat loaf and baked potatoes. You scrub the potatoes and I'll fix the meat loaf. Here's an apron." Just as if I was a part of the family.

After that, she had me set the table in the dining room. There was a big table, and we put a white cloth on it and set places for seven. It seemed like we were getting ready for a party, but Miss Stover didn't think anything of it. That's how it always was in their house, only that right now Mama was sick.

The sun was shining in the windows, and out in the yard the children were playing a game with wooden balls. Croquet, I found out it was. But Stevie wasn't playing. He was sitting in a big wooden swing that had two seats, and Skipper was next to him with his head in Stevie's lap.

I went out and said, "Hi! You having a good time?"

He said, "Uh-huh. This is a nice swing. You want to try it?"

I climbed in next to him and took Skipper on my lap, and we swung. It was a nice gentle swing. It went back and forth, back and forth, and all of a sudden I felt Stevie's head fall over against me. I put my arm around him and he went to sleep. Skipper jumped down, and I put Stevie's head in my lap instead, and there we sat, swinging back and forth.

The sun was going down, and I could hear some birds peeping, but everything else was just as quiet as it could be. It smelled nice, and there was a little wind blowing—not too much. You know, you could look at a picture of the country, or a movie, but you would never know what it was really like because you couldn't smell it or feel the wind.

Then one of the kids, I think it was Johnny, came over and said, "Mary says supper's ready." Stevie sat up and rubbed his eyes.

Then he said, "Oh hi! Where's Skipper?"

Johnny said, "He's in the house, eating. Come on."

The two of them raced into the house. It wasn't so quiet in there. The kids had the TV on, and Miss Stover was rushing around getting things ready.

She said, "Annie, will you pour the milk, please? And Stevie, I guess you'd better wash up. Johnny, show him where to wash and give him a clean towel. And Papa, would you tell Mama I'm getting her tray ready?"

Papa went in the bedroom all stooped over. But in a minute he was back, not stooped at all, and with a big grin on his face. He said, "Mama says she'd like to come to the table tonight."

And all the kids let out a yell, "Hooray!"

And Carol grabbed an extra knife and fork and plate to set Mama's place, and Billy got an armchair and put a cushion on it.

Miss Stover said, "Now children! Not so much excitement. You know Mama isn't very strong yet, so don't knock her over. Let's be pretty quiet."

Carol said, "Okay, Mary," and went and turned off the TV, and then Miss Stover said, "Come on, everybody."

"Here I come!" said Mama's voice from the bedroom.

Johnny and Carol ran and took hold of her, one on each side, as if they were afraid she would fall down. And she really did look kind of shaky to me, but she sat down at the end of the table and said, "My, it looks nice! I just couldn't stand the idea of eating in there all alone when there's company."

That meant Stevie and me, and it felt real nice to be called company.

Miss Stover said, "Johnny, it's your turn to say the grace."

Johnny said, "Father, we thank thee for the food and that Annie and Stevie are here and that Mama is up. Amen."

Miss Stover laughed and said, "That was short and sweet. Now back up your cart, everybody." And we all passed our plates for food and then started eating.

Mama asked the kids what they had all been doing, and then she asked Stevie about the train ride, and asked me about Grandma, and said she was sorry Grandma hadn't come with us, and maybe she would another time. I thought, wouldn't that be the day, if Grandma would take us visiting in the country!

But Miss Stover said, "We will fix it up, just as soon as Mama is on her feet again."

Papa didn't talk much. He just sat at the other end of the table and handed out meat loaf and looked pleased. He didn't have that awful bent-over look anymore.

Then Miss Stover said, "For dessert, you can have apple pie or ice cream. Take your choice."

Papa said, "I'll have apple pie with my ice cream," and then all the kids said the same thing. Carol got up to clear the table and I helped, and we brought in the dessert. Then Mama went back to bed and we all did the dishes.

I watched how Miss Stover did it. She had two

sinks, not one, and the soapy water was in one and the rinse water was in the other. And the kids were all lined up, some with towels and some putting away, and we did all those dishes in about half an hour. It was like a factory.

After that, we had to fix up beds for Stevie and me on the sun porch. I helped Miss Stover make the beds. She put extra blankets on them, because we might not be used to the cold. Then I thought, "If I don't get in one of these beds and go to sleep, I'll fall right on the floor."

Then Miss Stover said, "Time for bed, everybody." And there was a lot of fooling around, kids running around in their pajamas and brushing their teeth and throwing pillows at each other.

I thought, they have fun like this every night! I wished I could fool around too, but I was older than the rest, and besides I was dead tired.

So at last Miss Stover got them all in bed, and Stevie and me on the sun porch, and she came and kissed us good night. She turned out the light and said, "Sleep well, children," and was going out when Stevie sat up in bed and said, "Can't I have Skipper?"

Miss Stover said, "Oh yes! I promised you could." She called Skipper, and he jumped up beside Stevie and they curled up together. She said, "He may decide to go for a walk during the night, so don't be surprised if he isn't there when you wake up. Now good night."

54

Stevie said "G'night" in a sleepy voice, and Skipper gave a sigh that sounded like "Ooo-foo," and they were asleep.

But I lay there looking out through the screen. It was pitch dark, except for the light in the neighbor's window. I never saw it so dark. There were no street lights. Just the stars, twinkling far away in the sky. I could smell the cool night breeze and see the trees waving back and forth, and I thought, "I wonder what it's like to live in a place like this all the time. How do they go to school? How does the mother send the kids to the store? What's it like in winter?" I didn't know.

Remember What I Told You

THE NEXT THING I DID KNOW, THE SUN WAS SHINING right in my eyes, and Skipper had his elbows up on Stevie's stomach and was licking his face. Stevie said "Hi!" and grinned at me.

Boy, was I hungry! I jumped out of bed and put my clothes on. I could hear people getting up and water running, and I could smell the coffee.

Miss Stover said, "Good morning, Annie. Did you sleep well?" I said I did, and could I help?

She said I could set the table, only not for Papa and Mama. Mama was staying in bed, and Papa was out on his route. Then she said she would take the children to Sunday school and not stay to church, but hurry back so as not to leave Mama alone. I had an idea. I said, "Couldn't I stay with Mama, and you could stay to church?"

56

"Why, Annie, that's a lovely idea," she said. "I'll go and ask Mama if it's all right with her."

She said Mama was very pleased, and then she hurried to get dressed.

We had pancakes for breakfast, because it was Sunday. Stevie poured nearly the half of the syrup on his plate, but nobody yelled at him. After breakfast I had to wash him because he was all sticky. His good pants didn't look quite as good as yesterday, but I figured they would do for Sunday school.

Miss Stover put the chicken in a pan and told me to put it in the oven at eleven o'clock. Then they all got in the car and drove off, and there I was in the kitchen all by myself, except for Skipper. I gave him the bacon pan to lick.

Then I went and peeked in the bedroom to see if Mama wanted anything, and she was taking a nap. So I went back to wash the dishes. I remembered how Miss Stover did it the night before. I ran the water in the two sinks and stacked up the dishes. I put on an apron and put my hands in the soapy water, and then I thought, "This is my kitchen; it's my house. I live here, and all my children are at Sunday school." It was a funny feeling. I had to remind myself that it was only pretend.

After I finished, Mama woke up and I asked her did she want anything.

She said, "Do you think you could bring me a cup of coffee?"

I said yes, and she said, "You know how to light

the stove? Just put the coffee pot on to heat, and pour some in a cup with a little milk and a spoonful of sugar."

I did that, and then I saw a little tray and put the cup and saucer on the tray and took it in, and she said, "What a smart girl!"

But I thought I wasn't so smart; it was just the way the kitchen was fixed up, everything where it ought to be so you could find things. Grandma's kitchen is clean, but you have to look for things.

She said to sit down, and I did, while she drank the coffee and talked to me.

She said, "You remind me of Mary when she was your age."

I said, "I do?"

And she said, "Yes, she was always very bright and quick. Of course all my children were good children."

I thought, only I didn't dare say, that she and Papa were good too, and I bet they never yelled at the kids or hit them, the way Grandma did.

She must have been a mind reader, because she said, "You know, in a way it's easier to raise children that aren't your own; you don't get so upset when they're bad because you don't think it's your own fault. But when your own children are bad, you think, 'They must have got it from me, or from their father, and I must be real strict with them to knock it out of them, and I mustn't let them think I'm giving in.'"

I said, "I never thought of that before, but it sure does make sense."

Then she said, "But they're never bad to start with; it's just something that happens to them, and we have to try to make them forget it and learn how to live."

Then she said, "Did Mary show you how to light the oven?" And I remembered that I had to put the chicken in, so I ran and did that, and then I set the table for dinner. I put one of the plants in the middle of the table, and then Papa came in.

He said, "Well, look who's keeping house! Good morning, lady, would you like an extra bottle of milk today?"

I said, "Yes, please, because we have some extra kids staying with us, and you know how kids drink milk. But excuse me, I have to look at my chicken."

Then he went in to talk to Mama, and I went out and sat in the swing, and I felt so happy and peaceful, I just can't write down how good it felt. The only thing I wasn't happy about was, I wished we didn't have to go away. But then I thought, Mama is better, and probably Miss Stover will be back in school soon, and Stevie will be all right, and I'll see her sometimes.

Then there was the car in the driveway, and all the kids burst out of it, sort of like the car in the circus on TV, where a bunch of clowns come out, and more and more, and you wonder how they all got in the car.

Miss Stover called out, "How is everything?" And she rushed in the house and I rushed after her to help. We got dinner ready, and all the kids washed, and Mama came to the table again, and Papa carved the chicken and looked pleased.

Well, after dinner we cleared the table and stacked the dishes. The kids ran out to play, and Miss Stover called, "Don't go far, children. Stay in the yard." She said to me, "Now we must look at the timetable. I wish you didn't have to go, but we must think about trains." There was a train in an hour. She said, "I think you'd better take that one, so you get home before dark. Let's not wash the dishes, but just sit outside and rest till train time."

We sat in the swing, and then Miss Stover picked some flowers for Grandma and put them in paper. Then she called the kids and said, "Now Stevie and Annie have to go to the train. Who wants to go and see them off?" And they all yelled, "Me! Me!"

Stevie and I washed our faces and combed our hair, and said good-bye to Mama and Papa. Then we went out to the car. All the other kids were in, and I said to Stevie, "Get in," and he said, "No, I don't want to."

I said, "Come on, we have to go home on the train." But he said, "I want to stay here with Skipper."

I thought, "Oh, what'll I do with him now?"

But Miss Stover said, "Skipper can come to the

train too. Get in, Stevie, and take him on your lap." So he did.

We rode along the same country road the taxi had brought us on the day before. It hardly seemed possible it was only yesterday. Stevie didn't talk, he just sat hugging Skipper. We got to the station in plenty of time. There were some other people waiting for the train, with friends to see them off, and the friends were dressed in pants and sweaters and blue jeans, like Miss Stover and the kids. I thought, "Well, we didn't have anybody to meet us, but we have plenty to see us off."

Then we heard the bell clanging, and the gates across the road went down, and the train came whooshing in with a loud noise. Stevie gave Skipper a kiss right on the nose, and when Miss Stover said good-bye to him, he rushed over and hugged her around the waist.

She said, "Be a good boy now, Stevie, and remember what I told you." Then she kissed me and we got on, and all the kids waved and hollered, "Come back soon!" The train started, and we went faster and faster, flying past the houses and trees. We stopped at all the stations and picked up the people who had gotten off the day before, some with flowers and some with sunburned noses.

Then at last we were getting to the city. We saw apartment houses and sidewalks. I felt a funny thing, I mean not really funny, only I had never felt it before. I was *glad* to see the city. You see, out in the country I kept thinking if only we could stay there. And now I was thinking, "This is my place. I know the streets and the stores and where things are." Then I saw Stevie pointing out the window and saying, "Hey, we're almost home!" I guess he felt the same way.

Then the train slowed down and stopped, and we grabbed our flowers and jumped off.

It was Sunday afternoon, still light, and the street was quiet. There were church bells ringing, and a few people walking around with their good clothes on. We walked to our project and saw a couple of kids we knew. They said, "Hey, gimme a flower." But I didn't; they were for Grandma.

We went up in the elevator. As we went up, I could smell people's suppers cooking. Somebody was having roast pork and somebody else had cabbage. I heard a lady yelling, and a TV going, and a man laughing, and I wondered what was funny.

Suddenly I thought, "In a minute we'll see Grandma. What will I say to her?" I tried to get my key out of my pocketbook, but I couldn't find it. I was scared to ring the bell.

But Stevie wasn't. He rang it, and we heard Grandma's feet coming and her voice saying, "Who's there?"

Stevie hollered, "It's us, Grandma. Hurry up, I have to go to the bathroom!"

She opened the door, and he said, "Hi, Grandma!"

and shot past her. She shook her head and said, "That boy!"

I gave her the flowers and said, "Miss Stover sent them to you." She smelled them—I guess it was a long time since anybody gave her flowers—and she said, "Thanks, Annie," and put her hand on my head and smoothed my hair. Then she said, "You had me worried."

I said, "I'm sorry, Grandma. I guess I should have asked you, only I didn't think you'd like the idea."

She said, "No, I guess I wouldn't. You could have been in trouble. Thank God it turned out all right."

I could see she wasn't going to get mad. To tell the truth, I could have stood that better than if she said, "I try my best to raise you, and this is the thanks I get." But she didn't do that either. She just said, "Next time tell me. Now come on and get ready for supper."

She had the table set, and she looked for something to put the flowers in. We didn't have any vases, but she finally found a pitcher and put it on the table. Then Stevie came. He had washed his hands and face without being told. We had pork chops and fried potatoes for supper, and Grandma had bought a pie for dessert.

She said, "What did you have to eat there?" And when Stevie said we had pie with our ice cream, she said, "Wait a minute." She gave him some money and said, "Go down and buy ice cream, and we'll have it with our pie."

Then I told Grandma all about Miss Stover's family and the adopted kids, and what Mrs. Carter said about raising somebody else's kids, and she said, "There's a lot of truth in that."

And when Stevie came back he told about riding on the train, and playing in the yard, and swinging, and sleeping with Skipper, and going to Sunday school.

Then Grandma said, "I bet you wished you didn't have to come home." I said, "It felt good to come home," and she seemed to like that. She said, "Well, we can't live in a fancy house in the country, but we can be thankful for what we've got." I tried to tell her the house wasn't fancy, but she wasn't really listening.

After supper I wanted to wash the dishes the way Miss Stover did, instead of just holding them under the hot water. But we don't have but one sink, so I didn't know how to do it. So I let Grandma wash them and I dried.

Then we sat in the living room, and Stevie watched the Walt Disney film on TV, but I didn't bother. I sort of saw the screen like a bluish white window, but out of the real window I could see the other buildings in the project, with all the lights, and people moving around, and I could smell the warm summer air coming in. It smelled nice, not like country air, but a nice city smell that I was used to. Only it had a little bit of the trees and flowers in it. Maybe the wind brought it over from the park, or maybe all the way from the country, where Miss Stover was putting the kids to bed.

Suddenly I remembered something. I said to Stevie, "What did Miss Stover mean when she said, 'Remember what I told you'?"

He said, "Oh, she told me maybe she'd be back in a few weeks, and if Grandma would let us, we would have a picnic in the park and cook out, and take Skipper."

I said, "That would be fun. Gee, that Miss Stover has good ideas."

Then I remembered Betty, and I could hardly wait to tell her what we did. I thought, "She'll open her eyes when she hears this! Maybe I can bring her along to the cook-out. But I still owe her money, and how am I going to get it? I better try to do some baby-sitting."

Then I remembered another thing! I hadn't done a lick of homework! I said, "Excuse me, I have to do homework," and ran to my room. And I know it sounds funny, but I was glad I had it to do. I mean I was glad I had something that just belonged to me and didn't have anything to do with Stevie for a change.

Not Quite the Same

WELL, THE NEXT DAY WE WENT TO SCHOOL, JUST LIKE any Monday morning, but I felt excited. I wasn't the same person, because in between I had done something different, and all I had to do was remember it. Of course my teacher and the kids didn't know that; they treated me just the same. I was planning to tell all the girls about it at lunchtime, but then I changed my mind. I wanted to keep it private. Oh, I might tell Betty, but not the rest. I wanted to think about Miss Stover and the way she lived and what she said, and keep it all sort of wrapped up inside of me.

And I wanted to see if it would make any difference with Stevie. And it did. He played with the little kids and didn't tag around after Mike and the big ones. He was sort of relaxed, and you could

66

talk to him; he didn't act silly and run around and scream. He just acted like a nice little boy. And I didn't yell at him. I just told him what to do, but I didn't yell.

It even made a difference with Grandma. She treated me more like a grownup. It seemed as if she was thinking that if I could do that, why I might decide to do something else without telling her, and she better not yell at me too much.

I liked it and I didn't like it. Once you start deciding things on your own, you can't be a kid anymore. You have to keep on. "You're responsible," Miss Stover said. Then I thought, "Soon she'll be back, and things will be almost like they were before."

Then one day, after a couple of weeks, when I got home Grandma said, "There's a letter for you, Annie."

I said, "A letter? Who would be writing me a letter? Is it from some offer I sent away for?"

She said, "No, a real letter with a stamp on it."

So I took it and looked at the postmark, because there was no name to show who wrote it, and the postmark said Hacketsville.

I said, "It's from Miss Stover!"

You know how you read in books where it says, "She jumped for joy." That was what I felt like doing. I ripped it open and started to read. This is what it said:

Dear Annie,

I still think about the happy day you and Steven spent with us, and I hope you and your grandmother are well and getting along nicely.

You know I told you that I hoped to be back in school in a few weeks, and I was looking forward to seeing you and all my children again. But now I have to tell you some sad news. You know we all thought Mama was much better and would soon be on her feet. Well, we were mistaken. She took a turn for the worse and passed away three days ago.

It was a great shock to us, as you can imagine, and we will have to get used to not having her with us.

But for now, I won't be able to come back to the city, because the family needs me here. I wanted to tell you myself before you heard it in school, and I want you to know that I think of you and Steven often, and love you both. And I hope that one of these days, when things are a little more settled, you can come and see us again. The children and Papa send their love to you both, and so do I. I hope you'll write to me.

Your friend,
Mary Stover

Well, I could hardly read it to the end, my stomach hurt so. I didn't cry, I just hurt. The first thing I thought was, "Now I'll have the whole job to do myself." Then I thought, "I won't see her anymore," and it was the most empty feeling. In a way it's better not to love somebody than to love them and not be able to see them ever. Of course that isn't true, but that was how I felt. I ran in my room and lay down on the bed.

After a while I thought of Mrs. Carter and how much she liked the kids, and it was too bad she couldn't stay there with them. Then last of all I thought how the kids and Mr. Carter and Miss Stover must feel. It was a good thing for the kids that they had Miss Stover to take care of them. I thought, "They're lucky, and they don't even know it."

Grandma came in my room and put her hand on my head and smoothed my hair; it seemed like it was the only thing she knew how to do. But after a while she talked a little. She said, "I read your letter, Annie, and I know how you feel. But don't grieve too much. Miss Stover isn't dead, and you'll see her again."

So I said, "I don't know when I'll see her, and she was the only one who could manage Stevie. She was like his mother. I know you like us, Grandma, but it isn't the same as a mother."

I guess it was a mean thing to say to her, but she said, "I know, child, but look at it this way: it's good that you got to know her. Now look at me, I never knew my mother at all. I guess that's why I didn't know how to raise my children. But you had Miss Stover, and come to think of it you had your own mother. She loved you and your brother."

I sat up and stared at her. It was the first time she ever said anything about my mother that wasn't mean.

I said, "Well, if she did, why'd she go away?" I almost said, "Why'd she go and leave us with you?" But I'm glad I didn't.

Grandma said, "I don't know. Maybe it was just too hard for her, working and worrying about you kids. She was like a kid herself. She liked to have fun."

I certainly was surprised to hear her talk like that. I wanted to ask some more questions, but I could see she didn't want to talk about it anymore, so I got up and took a drink of water. There was that letter on the table, and something had fallen out of it that I didn't see before. It was marked "Stevie."

I opened it up and it was a folder with a picture inside. It was a picture of Skipper. It said, "Love to Stevie. Come and see me sometime."

So when Stevie got home I gave it to him. At first he didn't take in what it was. But then he woke up and said, "Hey! It's Skipper! Look, Grandma, Skipper!"

Then I told him what it said in the letter, and that Miss Stover wouldn't be back. He didn't listen at first, he was so busy looking at Skipper's picture.

But all of a sudden it sank in what I was saying, that Miss Stover's mother had died, and she wasn't coming back, and he began to get mad.

He said to me, "Don't you say that."

I said, "It's here in the letter," and showed it to him.

He said, "You're a liar!" And he balled up his fists to hit me, but I grabbed his hands, and he kicked and yelled and said, "She's coming back! She's coming back and she's bringing Skipper. She said so!" And he pulled loose and ran into the bedroom and slammed the door.

I thought, "Why did I tell him? I could have just let him have the picture." But then I knew I had to tell him, or he'd hear it in school and probably beat up some kid or kick the teacher or something.

I said to Grandma, "What should we do?" I think it was about the first time I asked her that, and I think it was because I knew she wouldn't hit him for acting like that.

She said, "Leave him alone for now, and then go in and talk to him."

I could hear him crying in there. But after a while he stopped, and I went in and said, "Stevie."

He said, "Get out of here."

But I sat down on the bed and said, "Did you see what Skipper wrote to you?"

He said, "No. What did he write? Hic!"

He gets hiccups when he cries hard.

I said, "See, he wrote, 'Come and see me some-time.'"

He said, "Go on, he didn't write that. Dogs can't write."

I said, "No, but he told Miss Stover to write it, and maybe sometime we'll go on the train again."

He said, "Hic! You mean it?"

I nodded my head yes. He was too little to think about Mama, or about Papa or Miss Stover, and how they felt. All he could think about was that he loved Miss Stover and Skipper, and couldn't have them.

He said, "When?"

I said, "Oh, when I save up enough money for tickets. And in the meantime you look out that you don't throw rocks at the train, or it won't be there when you want it."

And I wiped his nose and gave him some water for the hiccups, and left him sitting there looking at Skipper.

After a while Grandma made some supper and we ate it and went to bed, and the next day we went to school the same as usual, only I felt almost as if I had been sick and had been out a long time. I looked at Stevie, and he was walking along with his head down, and now and then he'd take a deep breath, and I thought, "He feels the same way."

So now everything is pretty much the same as before, but not quite the same, because as I said, we did this thing and it made us all a little different.

Stevie is still a pain in the neck, but not as bad as before. He quit going with Mike and playing hookey. He doesn't jump around so much; he'll even bring home a book from the library and read it sometimes, and he likes to draw pictures, mostly dogs and trains.

Grandma doesn't yell at him so much, and she doesn't hit him. I don't know if it's because he acts better—or does he act better because she's more patient?

It's funny the way you get over things like that. They leave an empty place, but then it gets filled up. For instance, I was in a play in school, and Grandma came. It took some work to get her to come. Then Betty's mother made a party for her, and I helped. That was fun. And I do baby-sitting. I like to take care of little kids, and maybe I'll be a teacher someday. I hope Stevie gets to do something good, like Miss Stover's brother.

Sometimes I think about Miss Stover, and wonder if she would like to be here in the city wearing that nice red coat and dress, or does she like washing dishes and cooking and taking care of the kids and the house? I wonder if her brother will come home and be a doctor there, and have her keep house for him.

Maybe someday we'll go to see her, but in the meantime I thought I'd write this down because I was thinking about it the other day, and some things I couldn't remember, and I thought, "I hope I don't forget it." And this way I won't.